BROTHERS
OF THE FALLS

Joanna Emery

Illustrated by Dave Erickson

SILVER MOON PRESS
NEW YORK

First Silver Moon Press Edition 2004
Copyright © 2004 by Joanna Emery
Illustrations copyright © 2004 by Dave Erickson
Edited by Hope L. Killcoyne

The publisher would like to thank Terry C. Abrams, President of the
Historical Club of the Tonawanda Reservation; Marion R. Casey,
Assistant Professor of Irish Studies, New York University;
and Sherman Zavitz, Official Historian, City of Niagara Falls, Canada.

For information:
Silver Moon Press
New York, NY
(800) 874–3320

Library of Congress Cataloging-in-Publication Data

Emery, Joanna.
  Brothers of the Falls / Joanna Emery ; illustrated by Dave Erickson; [edited by Hope
L. Killcoyne].-- 1st Silver Moon Press ed.
    p. cm. -- (Adventures in America)
  Summary: As the orphaned Doyle brothers leave Ireland to sail to the United States in
1847, thirteen-year-old James is accidentally separated from sixteen-year-old Thomas
and must make his own way to New York, find work, and somehow find his brother.
  ISBN 1-893110-37-0
  [1. Immigrants--Fiction. 2. Ireland--Emigration and immigration--Fiction. 3. Irish
Americans--Fiction. 4. Brothers--Fiction. 5. Orphans--Fiction. 6. Niagara Falls
(N.Y.)--Fiction.] I. Erickson, David, ill. II. Title. III. Series.

PZ7.E588Br 2004
[Fic]--dc22

                                                                              2003070376

10 9 8 7 6 5 4 3 2 1
Printed in the USA

For my parents, David and Elizabeth King,
who first introduced me to the Falls.

                                                    –JE

<u>ONE</u>

*I, Thomas Doyle, and my brother, James Doyle, soon
depart on this clear morning for our destination—America!*

TOM TAPPED HIS QUILL PEN ON THE
small ink bottle. "Should I write anything else,
little brother?"

"Two words," mumbled James, "horrible and
idea." He stared at the huge ship waiting in the
dock. The planks were old and worn, the ropes
frayed, and a long tear almost split the mast. He
didn't trust that ship. But he did trust Tom. When
their parents had died of the Black fever, Tom kept
his promise to look after James. With his muscular
arms and strong hands, Tom was a good laborer.
More than that, he knew how to write, taught by a
kindly priest back in Ireland. But neither skill made
any difference in Ireland where the potato famine
made any employment hard to find. "The Great
Hunger," they called it. Some even thought it was
God's punishment for the gluttony and waste of a
bountiful harvest the year earlier. James remained
unsure. He'd sooner blame the English than God.

Still, Tom was his younger brother's anchor.
"Don't fret," he'd say. "I can work anywhere." James

never thought that meant traveling to Liverpool to cross an ocean.

Tom tucked the paper and writing instruments into the brown leather satchel, grabbed his brother's hand, and pushed through the crowds.

"She may look like timbers strung together," said Tom, nodding toward the ship, "but she's our ticket to a new life."

He rummaged through the pockets of his breeches and pulled out two tickets. James glanced at the crumpled papers in his brother's calloused hands. He tried to read them, but his eyes began to water and the words jumbled in his head.

"I want to stay," James blurted out. "What if the ship sinks? Traveling from Dublin to Liverpool is one thing, but this . . .," he looked at the worn ship, ". . . this pile of wood and rope has to make it to the other side of the world!"

Tom spoke with his usual confidence. "She'll do fine. And so will you. You have more courage than you think. Try to be brave and strong."

James wished he were more like his brother. Tall, with chiseled features, a ready smile, and dark hair the color of polished wood, Tom was handsome—the opposite of awkward James and his own unkempt mop. But more than that, Tom never cried. Maybe once at the funeral of their parents. After that day, though, Tom never shed another tear.

They stood in line until the sun disappeared below the horizon. Finally, under an oil lamp's glow, the ship's officer read their tickets.

"Doyle. Two passengers to America—Thomas Doyle, age sixteen, James Doyle, age twelve."

"Thirteen," James interrupted. "My birthday was two days ago."

The brothers stood perfectly still, but the officer showed no sign of having heard James.

"You may board," he said finally, then held up one hand. "Where are your provisions?"

"Provisions?" asked Tom.

"Yes," huffed the officer. "Do you have food and supplies to last the voyage?"

Tom looked puzzled. "I understood that was included in our fare."

"Not here," said the officer stiffly. "Not unless you can survive on ship biscuits for seven weeks. And it could be longer if the winds are bad. You will need at least eight weeks' worth of food."

Tom frowned. "We don't have enough money to feed ourselves for two months." He glanced anxiously around the crowded ship. "And we don't have time."

"The captain is still on shore," said the officer. "'Tis safe to say we probably won't sail until tomorrow. You have time to buy provisions." He ushered them aside.

Tom took off the brown leather satchel and searched inside. He pulled out two small coins and said, "I'll go into town. I have enough money to buy a sack of potatoes. That should last our trip." He swung the satchel over James's shoulder and gently

shoved his brother up the gangplank. "I'll join you on board shortly."

James walked up slowly. He stopped briefly, gave his name to the arriving officer, and glanced behind him. Tom raised his hand through the crowd. James waved back, but he was worried, very worried.

An hour passed, then two. James sat on the deck's splintered wood. He fiddled with Tom's satchel and took out the journal. He couldn't write, but he could trace letters. Tom said that was a good start. He could practice, pour out his thoughts, and perhaps. . . Where was that ink bottle? Impatience had never been his vice, but today his palms would not stop sweating.

James grasped a familiar object. It was his sheepskin goat! Tom must have hid it in the satchel when he wasn't looking! Their mother had sewn it out of a sheepskin remnant shortly after James was born. Tom was forever teasing him about the goat. "Goats don't wear sheepskin!" he would joke.

Just before they left their farm, Tom had asked his brother if he were brave enough to go to America.

"Yes," answered James, "and to prove it I will leave behind my childhood toy." Now he was grateful Tom had known better.

"Down to the berths, boy," ordered the sailor.

James quickly closed the journal and stared up incredulously. "Births?"

The sailor raised one thick, bushy eyebrow.

"Berths. Your sleeping quarters. They're in the hull."

James followed the crowd of passengers through an open hatch and down a flight of creaky stairs. Several small oil lamps hung from the planks. James rubbed his eyes in the dim light. Rows of narrow berths lined each side of the hull. In one corner sat a plump lady with three noisy children clambering on her lap. She smiled at James, but he hurried past her and dozens of other passengers to the far end of the hull where he waited beside a barrel of dry goods. Once it was his turn James reached in and pulled out an oval-shaped biscuit. He tried to take a bite but it was as hard as a rock.

"This tastes like wood," he said, spitting out the crumbs.

"Unfit for animals," mumbled an old man with a toothless grin. James threw the biscuit back into the barrel and climbed into the first empty berth.

He took a deep breath and tried to relax. If he slept, perhaps Tom would be back when he awoke. James shifted uncomfortably. The lumpy straw mattress was scratchy and smelly. An itchy sensation crept up his leg. He glanced down to see two huge black bugs crawling towards his knee. Quickly, he flicked them off and clutched the brown satchel tightly against his chest. James lay motionless in the berth, his eyes glued to the wood planks above him, a mere arm's length away from the tip of his nose. He thought back to how he had tossed and turned for nights on end right after his parents died.

"Shut your eyes," Tom would say. "Pretend you

are asleep. That will help."

James let go of the satchel and stuffed it under his head. He closed his eyes tightly but after a few seconds they popped open. There were too many distractions. Babies cried constantly and a group of rowdy men were playing cards in the aisle. Sleep was impossible.

James turned onto his side and looked down the hull at the other berths.

"I am staying in New York," said a lady rocking a baby on her lap. "Will you travel on to Canada West?"

"No," answered the passenger across from her. "My sister lives in Lockport. I hope to find work there as a domestic."

"Papa," whined a small boy in the berth beside James. "Tell me again about the big waterfall."

His father held him close. "Niagara? I am told no one can tell about it properly because its beauty is so indescribable! But we shall try to find land near there and you may gaze upon its splendor each day."

James flung his head back on the satchel. New York, Lockport, Niagara—he knew none of these places. Tom had merely said that they were bound for America. Like so many others, they were leaving for a better life, a life far away from hunger and starvation.

Staring up at the ship's timber, James wondered how many wormholes were in the planks. Slowly, he began to count—one, two, three. At sixty-five, his eyes closed.

A quick jolt awakened James and he peered out of the berth. Tom was nowhere to be seen. Grabbing the brown satchel, he scrambled up the hatch.

"Thomas Doyle," he asked the first crewman he saw. "Has he boarded yet?"

"Later, boy, we're about to set sail."

James panted. "But he's my brother! Is he here?"

"The ship is full, lad," said the crewman. He hauled a thick rope onto the ship's slippery deck. "All passengers noted are now on board."

The ship was pulling out of the harbor! They were already leaving! James frantically pushed his way through the crowds.

"Tom!" he yelled. "Tom, where are you?"

A strong arm pulled him back and James came face to face with an imposing sailor. "Where are you going?" he asked, flexing his neck. "You should be down below with the others."

"I am looking for my brother. Is he on board?"

The sailor pointed across the deck to a group of passengers. "Speak to the arriving officer."

James pushed through the crowd to the officer holding a long paper and waited. Finally, it was his turn. "Thomas Doyle, my brother, has he boarded yet?"

"Doyle . . .," repeated the officer, ". . . hmmm . . ." He looked up and down the list several times. "I only see a James Doyle."

"That's me," James said, panic rising in his gut.

"Sorry, boy. There is no Thomas Doyle on board this ship."

Two

The Journey

JAMES FIDDLED WITH THE SATCHEL'S frayed strap and gazed out at the dark sea. Would he ever see Ireland again? Would he ever see his brother? He had asked more people than he could count if they had heard of the name Thomas Doyle. No one had.

A well-dressed gentleman approached, his red, blotchy cheeks puffing out as he hummed a tune.

"No luck, boy?" he asked in a posh English accent. He opened a silver snuffbox and tapped out a few specks. "Pull yourself up by your bootstraps and be strong. I was younger than you when I was orphaned."

James felt his nostrils flare. *He's probably never gone hungry like we Irish*, he thought and turned away.

As he trudged below deck, James noticed a burning smell had permeated the hull. He shivered. His throat tightened. In his mind's eye it was clear as day: the toughs who had been sent by the greedy English landlord. The torches the men used, setting the thatched roof on his family's cabin aflame. His mother's sobs as she clung to her husband, watching in agony as her home went up in smoke. Such were the tactics of evicting poor farmers who couldn't keep up with the rent. The painful image clear in his mind, James dashed through the aisle, almost knocking over the small cooking fire where a few passengers boiled potatoes.

"Aye, stupid youngin'!" shouted one startled man.

Heads jerked around and the yelling began. "Do that again," said an old woman sharply, "and you'll kill us all!"

James felt like every soul on board hated him. Dazed and too ashamed to apologize, he staggered back to his berth. He flopped onto the straw mattress and stared into the hull. *I hate them,* he thought. *I hate those English for what they did to our families and our land. And I hate everyone on this ship.*

"Eat this."

James wiped his eye. A dark-haired lady with a sleeping infant in one arm pushed a boiled potato in front of him.

"I 'ave been watching you." Her warm but reassuring voice reminded him of his mother's. "You must eat to stay alive."

He bit off a morsel. It was cold but soft and slipped easily down his throat. The kind-hearted lady was right. If he didn't perish on this horrible voyage, then perhaps there was a chance Tom would find him. He had to make himself believe that.

James steeled himself in his tiny berth. His stomach churned uncontrollably. A horrible taste inched its way up his throat. He sprinted up to the deck just in time to spew anything that remained in his stomach over the ship's side.

An old man placed a skeleton-thin hand on James's shoulder. "Seasick, boy?" he asked. James nodded his head. The man stank of brandy and soiled rags.

The awful sensation of nausea whirled inside his belly again. James spent most of that night on deck. When he finally went back to his berth, he lay completely still, only vaguely aware of the morning sunlight that seeped through the ship's hatch.

As the days passed, James noticed he felt less sick. But the ship had become increasingly foul-smelling. Fresh water was limited. No one could bathe or wash clothes. There wasn't even a decent privy around since the doors on it had fallen off. When the hatch to the above decks was open, every passenger breathed easier. If the weather was pleasant, some ventured on deck, trying to make the best of the situation.

Once James saw a white and black whale jump out of the sea. Another time, a gray porpoise followed the ship. He sketched them in his brother's journal after tracing a few more letters. Such moments lifted his spirits. His brother would be so proud.

If the waves were light, the Captain might permit the passengers to have a jig. A few would bring out their fiddles and those who weren't sick joined in song. The merriment continued until the officer shouted his usual, "Lamps out at ten o'clock!" Lulled by the ship's gentle rolls, most of the passengers would settle down for a restful night.

James rarely slept. He ached for Tom and yearned to set foot on solid ground. But the dry land he was heading for was a world away from his brother. Each day felt like a week and each week felt like a month. He rarely let go of the sheepskin goat.

As the weeks stretched on, James wondered if the voyage would ever end. He noticed that the jigs, the songs, even the conversation had gradually stopped. Apprehension was etched on almost every passenger's face. A few cried; others hummed to themselves. A group of women prayed the rosary, their voices echoing throughout the hull. Life grew miserable and passengers became ill. Ship fever they called it. A few even died and were buried at sea.

One night, as with most, James lay wakeful. He felt with uneasiness that the ship tossed more violently with each passing hour.

"Storm brewing," yelled a voice from the deck.

BANG! A heavy wooden box slid across the hull. It smashed against the opposite corner with a tremendous thud.

"Help!" screamed one passenger as he tumbled out of his berth. The ship heaved again.

"I should never have left home!" cried a frail old lady.

A nearby girl tried to comfort her. "Mother, I am sure the angels will protect us."

In the dark, the passengers clung to each other, to whatever they could. James mumbled a prayer, one hand firmly on the berth's side, the other clutching his sheepskin goat.

THREE

THE SHIP WAS MUCH QUIETER NOW. FOR nearly two months she had been filled with the sounds of children crying and sailors yelling orders. Now, instead of the constant roll of forward motion, the ship merely swayed gently in her port, creaking slowly while rain beat on the deck. She had reached America.

James pushed over his soggy mattress, its musty smell stronger than ever. The berths were empty; all the passengers had disembarked. Nothing was left but a few dirty tin cups and a small pile of rotten potato peels. He had survived on the few boiled potatoes the kind-hearted lady had given him to eat each day. That and those awful biscuits. No wonder he felt weak.

James pulled his legs up to his chest. He didn't have a penny. He didn't have any decent clothes or shoes without holes. He had nowhere to go and most of all, no one to go there with. He had the satchel and the journal, but he hadn't found the strength to sketch for weeks.

He was, though, alive. Half a dozen other passengers had not been so fortunate. Their bodies lay far beneath the waves at the bottom of the ocean. But dead, alive, or stranded on an empty ship, James saw no difference. He was completely alone.

A gentle warmth began to rouse him. As he lifted his eyelids, James realized it came from a lit candle. He instantly flung back his head and shielded his face with both arms. Suddenly, he felt a firm hand grasp his shoulder. "Calm now, lad. What's this fear?"

James slowly lowered his arms. Peering through his unwashed tangle of hair, he attempted to focus his eyes. A husky sailor with thick, dark eyebrows and a mouthful of chewing tobacco grinned back. Disoriented, James crouched farther into the corner of his berth.

"Don't want to get off the ship?" asked the sailor.

In a voice barely above a whisper, James answered, "Where could I go?"

"New York. She's outside, waiting for you. Didn't you hear the passengers disembark?"

Vague recollections of someone shouting, "Land!" followed by a bustling commotion returned to James. Was that yesterday? A few days ago? He remembered the kind-hearted lady asking him to accompany her off the ship. But James had refused. If he stayed on board, wouldn't the ship eventually return to Ireland?

"Where is your family?" continued the sailor.

"No family."

"A young one like you came alone?"

"My brother . . ." James gulped. "He did not board in time."

The sailor took James's bony hand. "What you need is somewhere to stay."

James knew there was nothing for it but to follow the man. He stuffed the sheepskin goat back into the satchel and followed the sailor to the deck. The rain had stopped, but James stepped directly in a deep puddle. Water instantly seeped through the holes in his shoes. A thick fog blanketed the surroundings. Tiny lights flickered in the distance.

With one forceful blow, the sailor spat out a chunk of tobacco. "You'll like America," he boomed. James said nothing, not wanting to say what he really thought. *I'll never like it. It will never be home.*

James shivered in his wet rags as he stepped off the ramp onto firm land.

"Hop in there," said the sailor, pointing to a waiting stagecoach. Despite the late hour, seven passengers were already seated on three wooden benches of the rickety wagon. The sailor squeezed in beside the driver, leaving James to scramble over the others.

"Ma'am's, again?" asked the driver in a Scottish accent.

The sailor laughed. "There's a pint in it for you, but who'll pay me?"

James clutched his satchel nervously as the stage jostled along the muddy road. He peeked through the flapping leather curtains at the rows of houses that lined the cobbled streets. After a brief ride, the wagon halted.

"Broadway Stage!" shouted the driver. Several passengers disembarked and boarded another wagon that sped off into a crowd of stagecoaches, livestock, and men on horseback. Lit only by a vast array of oil lamps and small warming fires, the street bustled with activity.

"Where are we?" asked James.

"Why, New York, of course," answered the sailor. "But we're heading to the countryside. Westchester County, just past the town of White Plains."

"I'm sick of travel," muttered James. He stared blankly as the stage continued towards a vast field dotted with large tree stumps. If Tom had made it to America, wouldn't he wait for him in New York, this country's largest city? But the sailor was taking care of him, and James knew, in his weakened state, it was more than he could do for himself.

Just before dawn they arrived at an imposing stone mansion flanked by a small barn, two gardens, and a wooden shack. A thick vine crept up one side of the mansion, its branches twice as thick as James's leg. Except for a few early songbirds, all was quiet. The heavy wooden door opened a crack. A pointy-chinned lady with silver hair peeked out.

"I've got another one for you, Ma'am," said the sailor. "Just in from Ireland."

The lady scowled. "Surely, one of the houses in town would accept . . ."

"T'was a bad voyage," explained the sailor, "and

what with city folks afraid of the ship fever and all, I've been given orders to take youngins way out here now. This poor lad got separated from his brother before the ship even set sail."

The lady put a wrinkly hand on James's shoulder. "Name?" she asked.

"James, ma'am."

She thanked the sailor stiffly, then pulled in James by his wet shirt and quickly shut the door. She told him to wait, briefly left the room, and returned carrying a wooden cup.

"Drink," she ordered.

James looked at the dark, watery liquid in the cup. When had he last eaten or drunk anything? As tasteless as it was, he finished it in less than a minute.

"We'll have to put meat on your bones," said the lady. "But first to bed."

James followed her up a steep flight of stairs to another large room. A sea of mattresses, each occupied by a sleeping child, covered the floor. One of the smallest boys, perhaps only three or four years old, opened his owl-like eyes for a moment, then fell back asleep. Newly arriving visitors were probably not uncommon. The lady showed James to a mattress directly under the window.

"Rest here," whispered the lady. "Breakfast soon."

"Am I in a boarding house?" asked James.

"Of sorts. Now sleep."

The lady left and James lay down. More than

once, the chorus of snores was broken by an ear-splitting cough and sputter, but only James remained awake.

He closed his eyes and shivered from a cold draft that snaked through the cracks in the wall. With each breath, James's nostrils almost froze. What would morning bring? Perhaps he could bathe, or would be given a new pair of shoes. Perhaps there would be word of Tom. Exhausted, James closed his eyes and clutched his little sheepskin goat tight.

Four

Peter, No Last Name

"YOU'RE NEW." JAMES OPENED HIS eyes to see the outline of a curly-haired boy above him.

"I'm Peter," said the boy. "No last name. Who are you?"

Still sleepy, James leaned on one elbow and held back a yawn. In the morning light he saw that the boy had dark blond hair. His blue eyes turned down at the corners, like Tom's. "My name is James Doyle," he replied, and then wondered why the boy was simply called Peter. No last name? James had never heard of such a thing.

Peter sat on his heels. "Irish aren't you? I can tell by the way you speak." He reached into his pocket and pulled out a half-eaten biscuit. "I saved this from last night's dinner, but you can have it."

James took a small bite. It was soft and buttery. "Better than the biscuits on the ship."

"Is ship food horrible?" asked Peter.

"Very horrible." James gulped down the rest of the biscuit.

"They don't let you wash, do they?"

"No," said James. *If my clothes are this dirty and smelly then my face must look worse!*

Peter pointed to a corner basin and pitcher. James got up, splashed the cold water on his face, and wet his hair down so it wouldn't stick up.

"A small improvement," commented Peter. "These might help too." He held out a comb in one hand and a clean but moth-eaten towel in the other. James ran the comb over his hair, but it didn't help much. He rubbed the towel on his face and dried off completely, behind his ears, his neck, and his arms. The towel turned almost black with dirt. James gave a low whistle of astonishment and sat back down.

"What kind of place is this?" he asked.

"An orphanage," said Peter. "Grown-ups call it 'The House of Refuge for Homeless Boys.' If you're lucky, a good family might adopt you. But they usually pick the babies first."

"And the older ones?"

"Boys must leave on their fifteenth birthday. Sometimes they are hired as laborers or farm hands."

"I'm only staying until my brother, Tom, arrives," said James

Peter frowned. "I hope he comes soon." He scratched his head. "What happened to your family?"

James swallowed audibly. "My parents died from the Black fever. We all got sick during the potato famine."

"Oh," Peter said, chewing a fingernail. "Well, take it from me, you don't need anyone anyhow.

When I was born my parents put me in an old basket and left me at the front door of this place. The headmistress said I was the smallest baby she had ever seen!"

"Left at the door?" James shivered. "Didn't they want you?"

Peter shrugged. "My parents put a note in the basket saying they didn't have enough money to care for me." He hesitated. "This is the only home I know, but I swore years ago that I would leave when the time was right. And I will."

DING! The clock chimed. Peter grabbed James's arm. "Hurry, James! Below stairs!"

They rushed to the lower floor and dashed into an open room. In the middle was a long table surrounded by dozens of boys quietly seated on matching wooden stools. James squeezed in beside his new friend. Within moments, a short lady in a plain black robe entered. Every boy instantly stood up and the lady commenced with the blessing. When she was finished, two plump ladies brought out trays of identical stoneware bowls.

"Mush again," mumbled a tall, gangly boy beside Peter.

James ate the hot, lumpy porridge so quickly it almost burned his throat.

Peter stirred his food. "In the spring they have maple sugar with this,"

James grimaced. "What kind of sugar?"

"Maple sugar. From the sap—the sticky water that flows out of a tree. You can make syrup out of it too."

James didn't believe him. "You're mad. Sugar doesn't come from trees."

"This sugar does," said Peter.

"Shh, not so loud," whispered an older boy next to them. He scratched behind his ear repeatedly. "I don't want extra chores, do you?"

"If we do something wrong, we're punished," explained Peter. "Chores usually, or prayers all day in the chapel. That, of course, is worse."

"Quick, quick!" barked a voice from the hall. "Stand at attention. We have a visitor."

James immediately stood up with the others. A stout gentleman in a black top hat entered. He nodded slightly and fiddled with a long, twisted moustache that matched his curly grey hair. He strolled up and down the tables, inspecting each boy as a general inspects his troops. Every now and then he glanced at the gold watch hanging on his waistcoat. It was the kind of watch only rich men wore. When he came to James and Peter, he stopped, smiled for a moment, then headed back to the hall.

"Remember what I said about being hired?" whispered Peter. "I thought the gentleman might do just that. Guess I was wrong."

"Perhaps he'll come back," said James.

"Can't count on it," said Peter with a sigh.

After breakfast, James, Peter, and the other boys cleaned their bowls in a large barrel of rainwater and placed them on the drying racks. The last one had just finished when Peter gave James a nudge. "Here comes the headmistress again," he muttered.

It was the lady with the pointy chin. She walked straight towards James and handed him a pile of clothes.

"Put this on, child," she said sternly. She did not move or show him where to change, so James faced the wall and modestly undressed. He gathered up the clothes and quickly slipped into the blue homespun shirt. Two buttons were missing near the bottom, but the shirt fit perfectly. The wool breeches, though, hung so loosely that the headmistress gave James a rope to tie around his waist. But the clothes were clean and dry, and a crackling fire warmed the room. For the first time in months, James's stomach no longer ached. Sadly, such was not the case with his heart.

By his third day at the House of Refuge, James had grown accustomed to the routine. He rose with all the other boys at six in the morning, washed at the pump in the yard, and then sat for breakfast. Chores followed. James pitched hay and fed the chickens, then filled the water jugs for dinner. They usually ate pork served with corn that tasted as sweet as barley sugar, both new to James.

In between meals were the lessons. As soon as the headmistress rang the cowbell, all the boys over the age of five rushed outside the main door.

"Two. Four. Six." From her spot beside a large pine chest, the headmistress counted heads. "Twenty-one, twenty-two. We will begin to write." She opened the chest lid and stepped aside. Each boy in turn took out a slate and piece of chalk.

James struggled to hold the chalk properly. He desperately wanted to learn, but this wasn't the quill pen and he wasn't permitted to trace words. It became too much. Tears welled up in his eyes. He hurled the chalk onto a flat stone where it shattered into dozens of tiny pieces.

A few nearby boys gasped. Fortunately, the headmistress had momentarily gone inside the main door and wasn't aware of James's actions.

"Look at us," sputtered James quietly. "We don't have a mother or father. We don't have money. We don't even know what will happen tomorrow."

Peter put his slate down on the ground, stared up at the cloudless sky, and said calmly, "I do."

"You do? What do you mean?"

"I know where I will be tomorrow. I will be far away. Tomorrow is the day I leave."

The words shot through James like an arrow. *Leave? Peter is my friend, the only thing that makes America bearable.*

"And this time I will succeed," Peter continued. "I tried to leave years ago, more than once. Each time some rich merchant or townsman who thought he was doing me a favor dragged me back to the orphanage. The last one had a better idea. He secretly told me to stay at the orphanage until I was older. 'If you can read and write,' he said, 'you can survive on your own. No reason for anyone to bring you back.' Last month, I knew I was ready. Tonight is a full moon and it will light my path to freedom." Peter grinned, the warm sun shining off his beaming face. Then he turned very serious. "Come with me, James," he said.

James felt his throat tighten again. "I only just arrived."

"You want to stay?"

"No, I . . . I don't know."

Peter shrugged. "I leave at midnight tonight. You have until then to decide."

The rest of the day was a blur to James. Peter confided that his plan was to run away to Niagara. There, he explained, the ocean tumbles from the sky. Or at least that was what he had heard.

That night, as James lay wakeful on his straw mattress, he saw Peter creep across the wood floor.

"Is it midnight?" whispered James.

"Almost," said Peter. "Are you coming?"

James gulped. "But how will Tom find me? I can't . . . what if . . . ?"

Peter put his hand on James's shoulder warmly, but he was not prepared for what-ifs. "Perhaps we will meet up again, James. I will remember your brother's name—Tom. Thomas Doyle."

James watched Peter sneak through the open window. Peter turned and waved. James swallowed the bitter taste in his mouth. "Wait!" he whispered as loudly as he possibly could. "I'm coming down too!"

He climbed out the window and steadied one foot on the vine's thick branch. Peter was already at the bottom when James suddenly stopped.

Tom's journal! My goat! I forgot the satchel!

"Wait!" he said to Peter. "I must get my satchel."

Before Peter could answer, James crawled back through the window. He scurried across the floor, grabbed the satchel beside his mattress, and was about to leave when the door to the sleeping area flung open.

"Master James!" scolded the headmistress. "What are you doing?"

FIVE

THE WEALTHY VISITOR

JAMES WANTED TO KICK HIMSELF. *I shouldn't have gone back. I'd be free by now.* Even though his heart still pounded, he sighed in relief that at least the headmistress hadn't noticed Peter's empty mattress. James had told her that he thought he had heard someone either enter or leave and had gone to peer out the window. "I grabbed my satchel," he explained. "I didn't want the thief to steal it."

The headmistress walked over to the window and shut it. "There's no one there," she scoffed, then abruptly left. But when Peter was discovered missing the next morning, the orphanage became a beehive of activity. The headmistress asked each boy what he knew. Each said he had not heard or seen anything, James included.

"You must have seen Peter near the window last night," she insisted. But James firmly denied it. Finally, the headmistress scowled, "Perhaps you'll remember over extra chores this evening, Master James."

By breakfast, the usual routine was back in place. James ignored his gurgling stomach and ran a finger over the bowl's rim. While the other boys ate, he stared blankly at the porridge. *First my parents, then Tom, now Peter. I am completely alone.* The headmistress's bellowed command interrupted James's thoughts. "You four, stand up!" she ordered, waving towards the boys on the end, James among them. "Follow me!" She led them down the hall into a large paneled room with heavy brocade drapes, a matching red carpet, and two wide black chairs. Next to one chair stood a gray-haired gentleman whom James recognized as the same wealthy visitor who had inspected them a few days earlier.

"Only these?" he asked. "I seem to recall a memorable blue-eyed boy with curly hair."

The headmistress wrung her hands. "He has . . . is . . . unavailable," she conceded, and immediately turned towards the boys.

"This is Mr. Green," said the headmistress. "He owns the Niagara Inn and has just arrived from Boston."

Boston? thought James. *Some of the ships from Liverpool docked in Boston. Perhaps this man has heard of Tom?* James ached to ask but held his tongue.

"Mr. Green needs a boy to work at his hotel," she continued. "Who would like to accompany him back to Niagara?" Every boy except James raised a hand.

"That Irish one just arrived from Liverpool," said the headmistress as she pointed to James. "I don't think you want him anyway."

"What is your name, lad?" asked the gentleman, ignoring her advice.

"James Doyle, sir."

"My dear wife was Irish," he reminisced. "God rest her good soul. She came from Sligo during the famine of 1821."

James was confused. The gentleman spoke in an English accent as thick and snobby as the snuffbox man on the ship, yet he had married an Irish girl. A rich Englishman with an Irish wife?

"Now my own sister has married a British subject," continued the gentleman. "Such a small world!" He stared at James. "You wish to stay at the House of Refuge?"

"My brother is looking for me," answered James.

"Yes, well," said the headmistress. "That could take months, perhaps years. Of course, he may not still be alive with smallpox so prevalent and all . . ."

"The orphanage will tell your brother where to find you," interrupted Mr. Green. He plucked a black pipe out of his coat but didn't light it. "I own the newest hotel in Niagara. Business is prosperous and the Falls are mighty popular. I need a lad to help in the stable and with general servant tasks." He briefly chewed on his pipe. "Do you wish to do that?"

James narrowed his eyes but did not answer. Thoughts raced through his mind. *Work for an Englishman? Father would roll over in his grave! But how can this man hate the Irish if he married one? And he is choosing me above the other boys.*

"I will pay you one dollar a month," added Mr. Green.

"One dollar?" repeated James.

"Raised to two if you work hard."

James's jaw dropped. *Two dollars? I can save enough money to go back to Ireland one day!*

The headmistress rolled her eyes. "My dear sir, the other boys are much stronger and . . ."

"I accept the offer," James blurted out. He straightened up even further. "You'll see how hard I work. I'll be earning my two dollars within the week."

Mr. Green chuckled. He tucked the pipe back in his pocket and pulled out a brown envelope, which he placed on the desk. "And a handsome donation for the orphanage while I'm at it."

The headmistress grinned like a fox in a chicken coop. "Finish breakfast first," she told James. "It will be a very long journey."

As the stage pulled out, James strained to catch a glimpse of whatever or whomever he could—Tom, Peter, anyone. But the towering trees soon thickened into a dense green wall that barely let a patch of blue sky peek through.

He sank into the smooth black leather seat of the luxurious stage. Its ride was still bumpy, but far more pleasant than the first wagon. There was more headroom and the top was solid wood instead of a cracked leather canopy.

Across from him, their knees almost touching, Mr. Green sat reading a newspaper. James scanned the cover for familiar letters, perhaps even the name "Tom." Nothing. He leaned his head against the side of the stage. Was Tom still in Ireland or somewhere in this vast, wild country? Was he even, as the headmistress had suggested, dead?

After the stage had stopped, Mr. Green and James boarded a speedy steamer that took them up the Hudson River to Albany. There they entered a local tavern which smelled of smoke, sweat, and ale. Around a large table in the middle sat a dozen burly men eating bread and cheese. Mr. Green paid for food and lodging, then joined the men. James waited on a corner bench, a wooden plate with his meal beside him. He chewed on a thick crust of bread and stared at the dark rafters, no doubt blackened by soot from the room's huge fireplace. A loud crack drew James's gaze towards the burning logs as they spit flames onto the hearth, inches from where he sat. Above the men's laughter, he heard words hollered in English voices— voices like those of the torch-bearing thugs who had come to his family's farm. Instantly, James was brought back to that day when everything he had known changed in the blink of an eye. James bristled with fear. Just when he felt he might dash outside, Mr. Green walked over.

"You're in luck," he said with a smile. "I've rented a room above stairs for myself, and there's a trundle bed through that door for you." He gestured towards the far end of the room. "Oh, and I thought you might need this." He handed James a slightly worn, red wool coat. "The Grand Canal gets mighty chilly at night."

James raised his dark eyebrows. "Grand Canal?"

"A triumph of mankind over nature. The canal stretches to the Great Lake Erie," explained Mr. Green. He patted James's scrawny shoulder. "Be proud of your Irish roots. The strong backbones of your countrymen dug most of the canal."

"My brother," said James. "He was . . . I mean, is as strong as the best of them."

Mr. Green nodded. "Sleep well. We board the packet at dawn."

SIX

A NATION IN CONSTANT MOTION

A SHARP ARROW OF A BOAT, *THE EVENING Star* packet was the length of a good-sized barn but only a fraction of the width. Unlike the freight-bearing line boats that shared the canal, both her bow and stern were pointed. "She can make five miles an hour," explained Mr. Green proudly. "The railroads are often faster, but this is a very pleasant mode of travel. Besides, I have time to rest, smoke my pipe, and catch up on my reading."

While Mr. Green descended to the private berth he had secured for himself, James remained on the vessel's narrow deck. He found a spot on the slender bench with dozens of other passengers. Packed like sardines, they could do little but talk, drink, or watch the dense forests pass by.

James studied the wiry boy who worked the tour path. *He must be only a few years older than myself*, thought James. It was hard to tell because a wide-brimmed straw hat concealed the boy's face.

"Fortunate lad," said a bearded man directly across from James. He reached under his fringed deerskin jacket and retrieved a small flask. "I hear canal boys are paid three dollars a month." He took a swig, then added, "All they do is keep the pulling mules in line."

A priest seated beside the bearded man broke in. "Those boys must ride or walk six hours a day and they are not paid until the end of canal season. I should think their employers would be more charitable in these prosperous times."

The trees broke into a wide clearing and a small town appeared. James stood up for a better view when someone shouted from the front of the packet. "Low bridge!"

His eyes on the town, James didn't notice the top passengers flattening themselves against the vessel. Suddenly, he felt a strong tug on his coat and was flung down backwards. A thick layer of stone instantly passed over him, mere inches from his nose.

"Almost knocked yourself into the water," said the man with the flask. James turned to see the solid stone bridge behind him. A few seconds later and he surely would have never seen Tom again.

After a five-day journey, Mr. Green and James finally disembarked at a town called Buffalo. Mr. Green surveyed a group of waiting stages before waving enthusiastically at one. "Penelope!" he hollered.

A young girl about James's age stepped out of the stage. She wore a fancy silk dress and her shiny light brown hair hung in curls like pork sausages. James's first impression was that she was rather pretty, but this observation was quickly dashed when she threw him a haughty look.

"My dear niece," said Mr. Green guiding her towards James. "Meet Master Doyle."

Penelope frowned. "Mother says I must not be friendly with the servants."

Mr. Green laughed and said something about his sister having changed since she married. "You may live in the town of Kingston in that British colony called Canada," he mused, "but remember, young lady, that you were born here in America."

As the stage wound along the trail, Penelope continued to ignore James. He stared out the window. Through a forest of giant beech trees he caught the occasional glimpse of the Niagara River. Its exquisite blue-green waters reminded James of his mother's eyes. He had finally dozed off when the ride came to an abrupt halt.

"Sir, are we being robbed?" he asked, eyes wide as saucers.

"Heavens no!" said Mr. Green. "We're merely stuck in the mud!"

Penelope laughed gaily until the driver ordered all hands out to push. James quickly learned that he was the only "hand" available. Penelope sat on a log and watched while Mr. Green complained of gout and offered to steady the horses.

"Perhaps the railroads are more efficient nowadays," he sighed.

"Yes, I love to travel on those iron horses," piped

up Penelope.

Neither the driver nor James said a word. After an hour of shoveling and heaving, the stage finally pulled free.

Caked in mud, James wiped his hands on his breeches. Mr. Green handed him a linen hankie.

"I'd give anything to wash up," said James.

Mr. Green smiled. "Well, it's getting late and the Falls look mighty pretty in the morning light. Let's stop for the night and get you fixed up at the next tavern." Penelope frowned at the delay, but true to his word, Mr. Green had the driver pull into the first tavern and paid for James to have a bath.

A bear of a man, the tavern owner led James around the back to a tin tub half full of rainwater. "This should warm it up," he said, pouring a pot of boiling water into the deep tub. "You're a lucky lad to have this luxury."

James ran a soap sliver over his tired skin. The hot water soothed deep into each sore muscle and dirt slid off his body like melted butter. He had never felt so clean. By the time he finished bathing, Mr. Green and Penelope had already retired to their rooms. The driver slept near the hearth, but James, wary of the still-roaring fireplace, simply lay down on his coat in a nook under the stairs.

Early the next morning the journey continued. While Mr. Green remained immersed in his newspaper, James tried to start a conversation with Penelope. "Ireland is greener," he said, "but your America has more trees." Penelope ignored him. James cleared his throat, conjured up a few choice words that summed up what he thought of her, and then returned to staring out the window. Stages full of passengers frequently passed by, some overtaking theirs with lightning speed. At one point James glimpsed a locomotive chugging along a stretch of railway. Back in Ireland, James rarely left his tiny village. Here, people thought nothing of traveling long distances. America seemed a nation in constant motion.

James suddenly noticed an unusual low rumble echo through the forests. The sound grew louder as they approached a strange white cloud hanging like a huge smoke plume in the distance. The stage rolled along closer and the sound gradually became a tremendous roar until finally, it appeared—the Falls—Niagara Falls—right in front of him! The "cloud" was actually an immense spray of turquoise water, plunging endlessly downward into a mass of white foam. It tumbled with a force more powerful than anything James had ever seen or imagined. Nothing back in Ireland compared to this spectacular sight. Speechless and almost dizzy from the view, he could not tear his eyes away from the breathtaking cascade.

As the stage followed the well-worn path beside the Falls, a wet mist gently moistened James's cheeks. Tiny water droplets hung in the air, thrown high by the Falls, creating a brilliant bow of colors that arched over the cataract.

"Ah," said Mr. Green. "I believe Charles Dickens himself said it best during his visit a few years back: 'What heavenly promise glistened in those angels' tears.'"

James felt as if he were in a timeless world, gazing forever on the most beautiful and mighty creation nature had ever produced. But it wasn't all nature. Newer buildings, scruffy shacks, and a strange round tower stood right near the brink of the giant, horseshoe-shaped Falls. Several mills had also sprouted up along the river shore. James had seen their like before, in Liverpool, teeming with worn-out workers.

"Progress," commented Mr. Green. "Good for business. Good for us all."

"Poorer folk should be grateful for those jobs," Penelope said haughtily. Before James could respond she changed the subject. "Uncle," she asked. "What would happen if someone tried to swim over the Falls?"

"I don't know if anyone has tried to swim over them," answered Mr. Green. "But years ago a man named Sam Patch dove into the river."

James broke in quickly. "He survived?"

Penelope frowned at the interruption but Mr. Green did not hesitate to answer. "Only to perish in another stunt a fortnight later," he said. "I was there, at the Genesee River in Rochester. Sounded like a fired musket when young Mr. Patch hit that water." Mr. Green imitated with a clap of his hands, then chuckled. "Stunts are good for business too."

"There," said Penelope pointing out the window,

"that's the Niagara Inn, Uncle, isn't it?"

Not far from the Falls stood a magnificent manor. It dwarfed the smaller inns they had passed. As they neared it, James noted that the Inn reached as high as the tall ships of Liverpool, with seven elegant wooden columns guarding the facade. The stage headed around the back to a long brick stable surrounded by freshly tied bales of hay.

A servant scurried up. "Good day, sir," he said collecting the luggage. James followed the party towards the main house until Mr. Green abruptly spun around.

"Sorry, lad. The servant's quarters are below. Mr. Hodge, my manservant, will come and show you."

Embarrassed, disappointed, and angry, James stared blankly into the distance as he waited for this Mr. Hodge. Horse trots echoed across the courtyard and a newly arrived stage came into view. Three guests stepped out—two fashionable ladies and one tall young man with a familiar gait and wavy, chestnut-colored hair. Hair the color of polished wood.

James blinked in astonishment. "Tom!" he instantly hollered. "Tom, you are here!"

SEVEN

JAMES, THE SERVANT

"I BEG YOUR PARDON?" THE WAVY-HAIRED man's steely gaze seared through James.

"I, I thought you were my brother," James explained.

"Rather impudent of a servant to think that, wouldn't you say?" he scoffed.

James searched for a polite answer. "Well . . . I . . ."

The man brushed some barely perceptible dust off his jacket sleeves. "I suppose I shouldn't expect much from an Irish servant such as yourself anyway."

James bristled at the man's rudeness, a man who only moments earlier he had thought was his beloved brother. James was about to tell the disgruntled stranger that he could go and take a dive into the Falls when a pair of bony hands swung him around. Mr. Hodge, the manservant, had intervened.

"There you are, lad," said Mr. Hodge, still firmly grasping James's shoulders. "Now let me take you to your proper place at the stables where you will receive full work instructions." He nodded at the wavy-haired man. "Please forgive the interruption. The boy recently arrived from an orphanage. Of course, he will be dutifully reprimanded."

The man sneered, and with a toss of his head marched towards the main entrance. James clenched his teeth. It was a rocky start to a new life.

One month to the day of his arrival at the Inn, James knew his lot hadn't improved much. Rules were hammered into his head like horseshoe nails. He was to follow orders without question. He was not to speak with Mr. Green's family or the guests unless asked and he must never, ever, raise his voice. He was to sleep in the straw loft, not below stairs in the main house with the higher servants. In other words, James was at the bottom, the lowest of eight servants, and the only one from Ireland.

One hot and humid day, as the other servants sat down at the long table for the noontime meal, Mr. Hodge delicately patted his lips with a napkin and stood up. James always thought Mr. Hodge, rail-thin with a somber expression, could have passed as one of the sickly old men from the immigrant ship.

"I wish to remind you," announced Mr. Hodge, "that Mr. Green is expecting guests for dinner."

"Who is invited?" asked James, wondering if the name "Tom" might by some small chance be raised.

"Servants must not ask such personal questions," Mr. Hodge chastised.

Cook rolled her eyes. "Yes, we know, Mr. Hodge," she interrupted. "Now, James, finish your dinner, then fetch more logs for the fireplaces."

After polishing off his meal, James excused

himself, placed his dirty plate in the scullery, and trudged out to the woodpile. He collected an armful of logs, dropped them beside the hearth, and proceeded to finish his stable chores.

James pitched each shovel of hay as if it weighed a hundred pounds. It wasn't that his tasks were too difficult; he did all he was told. He simply did not like performing such tedious, mindless work. The stifling summer heat didn't help. Exhausted, he leaned on the half-gate and wiped his brow. It was then that he caught a glimpse of Penelope skipping under the shade of a tall elm tree and singing to a small white dog.

Here we can play so free and happy. Stay with me, my little puppy.

She stopped suddenly and scooped up the dog. James shuddered as he watched her march towards him. The dog's furry head peeked out from her folded arms. "Uncle says you groom the stable horses. Do you?"

James nodded.

"Can you groom my poodle, Fritz?" She glanced toward a soot-mark between her pet's ears. "He gets into everything and his fur is rather messy. I want him to look pretty for the dinner this evening."

"Your uncle won't mind?"

Penelope cradled Fritz like a baby. "Of course not!" she gloated smugly. "If you must know, he has no idea. He's busy in the study reading his papers and smoking that pipe of his. But you shouldn't even be asking me such a question!"

She handed him the dog and strutted back toward the house. James bit his tongue, holding himself back from telling her that what really needed grooming were her manners. He was quite sure the next time his tongue wouldn't stay so neatly bitten. He was rather looking forward to it.

Fortunately, Fritz was a gentle animal. His little tail wagged as James bathed him in the old soapy laundry water and dried him with a small horse blanket. He pulled a wooden hair comb out of his pocket, the one Peter had given him, and carefully untangled the dog's white fur.

When he was done, James proudly walked Fritz into the courtyard. Cook scurried past with six plucked pigeons dangling from her hands.

"There, do you like it?" asked James.

"Miss Penelope's dog!" gasped Cook, almost dropping the birds. "What are you doing with him?"

"She asked me to groom him for this evening."

"You had better get that dog back before Mr. Hodge catches you. He'll whip you sore for speaking with Miss Penelope."

James walked back to the porch but Penelope was not there. Muffled voices floated through the half-open door. James peeked in and decided he would have to put the poodle inside the house where, he hoped, Penelope and Mr. Green would find the pup. The floor was covered in square burgundy tiles. Large portraits hung on the mustard-colored walls. In the center of the hall, a huge, spiral staircase towered upwards. A few guests milled around the bottom. James tiptoed towards the first open room and gently lowered Fritz down. He cuddled the dog affectionately. "I'm going to miss you, little fellow," he said warmly.

"Fritz!" he heard Penelope shriek. She bounded from behind the doorway and crouched to Fritz's level. The fluffy puppy leaped into her arms. James stood there while Penelope got up and turned away without so much as a thank you.

"There goes," James muttered under his breath, "one of God's sorrier creatures."

The lavish dinner menu was so extensive that more servants were required, so Mr. Hodge ordered James to put on a new outfit and assist. James was happy for the change of clothes, which fit him perfectly.

Each porcelain plate held a tempting delicacy: roasted duck and pigeons, boiled ham, jellied veal, giant oysters, pickled asparagus, and an assortment of fruit. The warm evening air was a feast of exquisite aromas. James couldn't wait to taste the leftovers he and the other servants had been promised.

"Stay there," whispered Mr. Hodge as he ushered James to one corner of the dining room. "If the guests require anything, they will wave for you."

James wasn't going to wait idly. Perhaps the guests knew Tom? Surely one of them might have heard his name. But servants must be quiet. Still, he could listen to their conversation.

"Yes, darling," said a lady in a fancy black lace dress. "The Falls are magnificent. Actually, there are two cascades. One shimmers like the lace of a bridal veil. The other resembles a giant horseshoe."

Another gentleman turned towards Penelope and asked, "Did you read about the Grand Caravan in last week's *New York Herald*? The exhibit will be on our side of the Falls this Saturday. You must go and see the wild beasts from far off Africa, Miss Penelope. Lions, tigers, monkeys—it will be such a delight."

James shifted nervously beside the wine bucket. The half-full bottles were still open and the strong fermented smell left James light-headed. A sharp voice beckoned from the end of the dinner table. "More wine, young man!"

James carried the heavy bottle across the room. As he attempted to refill the glasses, he felt his head spin and accidentally leaned sideways, knocking over a lit candle. The flame scorched James's shirtsleeve. Panicked, he screamed and leapt backwards, causing the wine to splash into one gentleman's face.

"My goodness!" shrieked the man's wife. "I have never . . ."

"Calm down, Prudence," interrupted the gentleman, wiping at his forehead. "It's simply a tipped candle and a little spilled wine. No harm done. I am sure the boy is very sorry and quite embarrassed already."

But James hadn't stayed around to apologize. He was already at the scullery cradling his slightly blistered but otherwise unharmed arm in a pot of cold water, tears streaming down his face.

EIGHT

THE GREAT FALLING SHEET OF WATER

CLANG! CLANG! COOK BANGED A WOODEN spoon against the iron pot.

"I'm here," sighed James as he plodded into the kitchen. He plunked a basket of turnips on the long wooden table. "I could hear that banging from the garden."

"Wonderful turnip-picking, James," Cook said with a smile. "Mr. Hodge wants to see you."

James stooped down to pick up a few turnips that had tumbled out. "First stable chores, then turnips. It never ends, does it?"

Cook playfully tousled his messy hair. "Remember your pay. It's a step closer to finding your brother."

"I suppose," said James. He grabbed a damp cloth and tried to wipe the dirt off his hands and arms. He scrubbed hard but the soiled stains remained.

A familiar voice echoed from outside. "No time for that." James pivoted in his boots to see Mr. Hodge stride through the door.

"Come now," said Cook. "The lad simply wants to be presentable."

"Orders are orders," Mr. Hodge replied flatly. "James, you must go to the stage immediately. Mr. Green requires you to carry picnic supplies for their outing to the Falls."

James couldn't believe his ears. He was going on a tour of the Falls! True, it was work, and the wretched Penelope would no doubt boss him about, but he would finally see the famous Falls up close. What's more, the place teemed with tourists. Perhaps Tom would be there!

Penelope stood beside her uncle. "If only the head servant boy hadn't become ill," she pouted. "He was much more polite, not as filthy, and he didn't carry around a stupid satchel."

Mr. Green helped his niece into the stage. "We need someone to carry the basket for us on our excursion around the Falls," he explained. James dutifully picked up the large wicker basket, climbed into the stage, and set the basket between his feet. Penelope sat directly across from him, her gloved hand covering her nose.

After a short jaunt, the stage stopped at a footbridge that crossed the Niagara. On the other side was Goat Island—a lush, green oasis in the middle of the swift river. Mr. Green pulled out a book from his breast pocket. He scanned the pages until he found what he was looking for. "Ah, here it is."

"Is that the new book from Buffalo?" asked Penelope.

"Yes, dear," answered Mr. Green. "It is called *A*

Pictorial Guide to the Falls of Niagara Giving an Account of This Stupendous Natural Wonder and All Objects of Curiosity in the Vicinity." Mr. Green placed his finger on one passage. "Says here that goats once roamed this island. The name stuck even though visitors have replaced the animals."

"After we eat, Uncle," said Penelope, "I want to go up that strange Terrapin Tower."

James fiddled with the basket's woven handle. *Penelope's favorite words*, he thought, *"I"* and *"want."*

Once they were across the bridge, the small party settled on a nearby rock overlooking the rapids. James laid out the cloth, cutlery, and food from the picnic basket. While Mr. Green and Penelope nibbled on chicken legs, James carried an empty jug to the river's edge. As he filled it with cold water, he noticed letters etched on the rocks and trees around him. They seemed to be words, perhaps the names of tourists who had visited the Falls. James set down the water jug and scoured the marks but could not find any that made the name "Tom." His heart sank. He didn't want to admit it, but part of him was beginning to wonder if finding Tom in this vast country would be as impossible as trying to stop the Niagara River from rushing over the Falls.

After lunch, Mr. Green and Penelope walked up Terrapin Tower. As he waited, James ambled in the nearby brush and picked up a long branch that resembled a walking stick. Before he could try it out, the two immediately came back down.

"Those stairs creaked horribly," Penelope complained. "If we stayed any longer, I'm sure that tower would have collapsed. I want to cross over to Canada and visit Table Rock instead, Uncle."

"We will have to go down to the *Maid of the Mist*," said Mr. Green. "She'll ferry us across the river."

James enjoyed the short sidewheel steamboat ride to the Canadian side of the Falls. Once there, they headed up towards the flat stretch of cliff called Table Rock that jutted directly out to the cascade. Dozens of people milled about, braving the gusty winds and sparkling spray to admire the Falls. James leaned on his stick and studied the visitors. One man sat on a stump and sketched scenery. Another strolled by, an elegantly dressed lady at his side. At the far end, near an old shack, three Indian women in unusual clothes sold crafts of baskets and beadwork. Despite the Fall's roar, James could hear that they spoke in a strange language.

Penelope's shout broke his concentration. "That's a silly name, Table Rock."

James shook his head. *The ninny! Couldn't she see that this large part of the cliff stuck out like a flat table?*

They lingered near the crest and watched the water plunge well over a hundred feet down. James steadied himself with the stick as the wind whipped through his clothes. The cascade created such a powerful, hypnotizing force that James thought he was floating, as if in a dream. Without turning his eyes away, he heard Penelope ask her uncle, "Isn't it dangerous to stand so near the precipice?"

James instantly felt some loose earth crumble beneath his feet. Before Mr. Green could answer, he broke his gaze and leapt backwards. His walking stick dropped into the rushing water, plunged over the Falls, and whirled through the torrent until it disappeared.

"Be careful!" screamed Penelope.

By now, James had stepped several feet back to safety and watched the horrified expression on Penelope's face change to one of relief, then indignation.

"Why don't we proceed to the tour," said Mr. Green as he hustled the two away. "Master Doyle, run up ahead a quarter mile and fetch the Indian, Kit. He's the best guide around."

James suddenly remembered stories from the ship, frightening tales of wild savages. "I have never spoken to an Indian," he said.

"You will now, lad," said Mr. Green.

James poked along the woodsy path, nervous, but also curious about meeting an Indian. The brush soon gave way to a small clearing where a rough log cabin stood directly in the middle. Not much bigger than a privy, the makeshift cabin didn't even have a door. Instead, a dusty yellow blanket hung over the entrance, in front of which sat a man on a tree stump. He had dark skin and long, straight black hair that stood out against a bright blue shirt. His leggings were decorated with beadwork and his shoes were made of a soft beige animal skin fitted with tie-strings.

Closer up, James noticed deep pockmarks on the Indian's face. He had seen the same marks found on smallpox survivors in Ireland. He tried not to stare.

"Are you Kit, the Indian?" he asked, then immediately took a step back. Perhaps the Indian did not want to be disturbed. Perhaps he had made him angry. "I am sorry . . ."

The Indian smiled gently and tugged at the side slits of his loose homespun shirt. "In your language, my name is Kicking Deer. The tavern owner and his business partner, Mr. Green, thought 'Kit' was a better name for business. Is Mr. Green your employer? Did he ask you to look for the Indian?"

James nodded quickly.

"I am O-non-dowa-ga," Kit added.

James's eyes widened. "What is that supposed to mean?" The strange syllables tumbled around in his head.

"My ancestors came onto earth from the chosen spot, a hill near Lake Canandaigua." Kit made a heartfelt bow that soothed James's nerves. "Come," he said, gesturing down the path, "I will tell you while we walk back to the tour."

As they trekked down the trail lined with trees that slightly muffled the cascade's roar, Kit told James about his people and how they believed that no one should be richer or poorer than another. Intrigued by this notion—the very rightness of it— James soon found himself walking side by side with the Indian until they arrived at a building near Table Rock where Penelope and Mr. Green waited.

"Now we can finally go on the tour," said Penelope excitedly, "and get a certificate."

"Let's proceed," answered Mr. Green.

As he followed them into the building, James asked Kit privately, "What's this about a certificate?"

Kit nodded slightly then, while Mr. Green and Penelope looked around, he stepped into a closet and re-emerged with a long tin box. He opened it, took out a stack of loose papers, and read off the top sheet.

"This may certify, that M _____
Has passed behind the Great Falling Sheet of Water to "Termination Rock."
Given under my hand, at the Office of the General Register of the Names of Visitors at the Table Rock, this _____ *day of* _____ *of 1847."*

"So those are the certificates," said James. "The ones you give to visitors who take your tour and touch Termination Rock."

"Or look as though they have," chuckled Kit.

"You must make a fortune with the tour."

"Not that much," answered Kit. "I give most of what I earn to my people, the People of the Longhouse."

James was intrigued. "Tell me more."

"In time," said Kit. "But first, the tour."

By now, Mr. Green and Penelope were ready. Kit

gestured towards a back entrance and spoke in a loud voice. "The stairs will lead us down to Termination Rock. It is a brave person who crosses the slippery stones behind the Falls to touch the Rock." He pointed to a pile of dingy beige capes. "These oilcloths will keep you dry." James was about to step forward when Mr. Green stopped him.

"Why don't you wait here," he said, "and guard our things."

James bit his lip. Every muscle in his body tightened until he was as rigid as a statue. He watched Mr. Green and Penelope put on their oilcloths and descend the staircase to the base of the Falls. It seemed like forever until they reappeared and came indoors, their hair and faces drenched from the bone-chilling spray. The oilcloths hadn't kept all the water off their clothes, but no one complained.

Penelope held up her certificate and sang, *"Look at me, a young lady, who completed the thrilling tour!"* Mr. Green thanked Kit and gently ushered his niece and James outside. As they headed away from the tour, Penelope fussed with her soaking wet hair. "Oh no!" she cried. "My pink bow! It must have blown off in that cave wind." She immediately turned to James, "You *must* find it. It's pure silk. I can't bear to lose it."

"Yes, be a good lad," added Mr. Green. "Return to the tour and see if it's there. We'll wait for you at the Signature Album near the Table Rock building."

I don't want to search for a silly bow, thought James. *And I don't remember any Signature Album.*

Reluctantly, he jogged back to the tour.

By now, Kit was flattening out the oilcloths to dry. He glanced up, reached behind him, and pulled out the lost bow.

"Miss Penelope ordered me to fetch it," said James sourly.

Kit chuckled. "Women are very powerful, but remember life comes from them, from the Sky Mother."

James pricked up his ears. "The Sky Mother?"

"Some call her Sky-Woman," said Kit. "She bore twin sons, Good Mind and Evil Mind. They fought with each other until Good Mind finally triumphed."

James gasped. "He killed his brother?"

"Banished him," explained Kit as he thrust a fist towards the ground. "Banished to a pit under the earth."

"Thank heavens," said James.

Kit held up one finger. "But," he continued with a glint in his dark eyes, "Evil Mind has servers that can assume any form and still wander the earth."

James pondered the story for a moment. *Brothers. I miss my own brother.* "I should go back," he sighed. "Penelope and Mr. Green are waiting for me at the Signature Album, whatever that is."

"Ah," said Kit. "That leather-bound book on its rickety pedestal is more precious than they realize. I tell all the visitors to go there and write down their thoughts about the Falls."

"All visitors?" repeated James. Like a lightning bolt, the thought flashed through his mind. "I must see it!" he exclaimed and raced off.

Nine

The Grand Caravan

JAMES GRABBED HIS SATCHEL AND WALKED across the courtyard. Another outing, at Mr. Green's request, with Penelope. His first thought was of last week's disappointment. *Tom's name was not in the Signature Album. Perhaps I can search again today, or even see Kit.* He ran a hand through his hair and moaned. America had grown uncomfortably hot. It was only mid-morning but beads of sweat already collected on his brow. Several yards away, beside a waiting stage, Penelope was speaking with her uncle. James watched her arms flail in circles like some sort of large, upset bird. He snickered. No doubt her temper was about to rise as fast as the summer's heat.

"Why must James be my escort?" whined Penelope. "He smells like the stables and never washes his hands."

James cleared his throat. Penelope swung around. For a brief moment she seemed rather mortified that he had overheard her comment. *Maybe she has a shred of humanity in her after all,* he thought.

"You do want to see the Caravan, don't you, my

dear?" replied Mr. Green. "Besides, I have business until late this evening." He fished a few coins out of his breast pocket and handed them to James. "There's more than enough here for the entrance fee," said Mr. Green. "Do keep a watchful eye on Penelope. I trust you."

James slid over the stage's black leather seat and brushed against its velvet wall, still thick with the odor of stale pipe tobacco. Why did Penelope have to protest so much? She was truly a royal pain in the backside.

He pulled out the pocket comb and tried to smooth down his hair, but the strands still stuck upright. Penelope frowned with disapproval. She turned her head and kept it there for the rest of the journey. James peered out the small window. Dozens of stages, horses, and people crowded around the entrance of a gigantic green tent.

When they arrived, James found himself shoulder to shoulder with the crowds in front of the tent. He was reminded of all the passengers he and Tom had pushed through to board the ship at Liverpool. But this atmosphere was different. There were no half-naked, ragged families here. Children laughed in anticipation, they did not cry with fear.

A gust of wind blew through the tent. As the line inched closer to the entrance, a wild musty smell enveloped the customers. Just before their turn, Penelope demanded her share of the money.

"I can do it myself," she told James. He obliged and she dropped her coin into the hand of a surly attendant with a bulbous red nose.

"Go on in," barked the attendant. "But don't let the owner catch you touching nothing!"

She shot him a piercing look and disappeared under the tent flap. James followed, trying not to slip on the straw strewn over the ground.

"Monkeys!" squealed Penelope as she pushed her way through the other customers.

Before James could catch up, Penelope was already at the next exhibit, an iron cage holding a lion and lioness. James stopped near a small cage crammed with half a dozen thin wolves. Saddened at the animals' plight, he turned around, only to see a most unusual creature.

"What on earth is this?" James asked aloud. Something like a tall orange cow with black splotches and a long neck towered motionless over him.

"It's a giraffe," chided Penelope, already back from the lion cage. "I have a picture of one in a book." She tugged on the giraffe's tail. "Stuffed." she grumbled.

James thrust out his hand. "Don't touch it! Remember?"

"I do what I wish," announced Penelope. "Anyway, I paid to see live animals, not stuffed ones!"

James circled the giraffe and peered through its long legs. A small boy dashed by from behind and inadvertently bumped one of the giraffe's front legs. The animal began to rock but James immediately grasped both legs and steadied it.

"What are yer up to?" growled a deep voice. "Get away from the exhibits!"

With both hands still steadying the giraffe, James looked up to see the Caravan owner. "Sorry, sir. I was trying to . . ."

Angry, the owner glared at James. "Irish, aren't you?"

"Yes, sir," said James.

"Yer Irish is nothing but trouble," he muttered.

James let go of the now stable giraffe and straightened up. The owner spat out a wad of chewing tobacco. "Yer come here like scrawny swine bringing the fevers and all! Nothing but thieves and beggars yer Irish is!"

James exploded. "Enough!" he shouted and instinctively threw a punch.

The Caravan owner tumbled into a bale of straw. "Why yer dirty little Mick!" he screamed, struggling to get up.

Momentarily stunned that he had actually struck the Caravan owner, James stood motionless, oblivious to people who had gathered around. "Serves you right!" he finally blurted out. "Bet you won't even remember when you're sober. More's the pity."

Out of the corner of his eye, James glimpsed the purple swoosh of Penelope's expensive silk dress. "C'mon," he said, grabbing her arm. "We're getting out of here!"

"Let go!" Penelope protested, but James pulled her out of the tent. He half-dragged her past the waiting stages and didn't stop until they were safely behind a dense thicket.

"I'm sorry, Miss Penelope," he said panting. "But

I would not be much of an escort if I were lying unconscious in the Caravan."

Penelope straightened her sleeves. "You're a horrible, good-for-nothing ruffian! Just wait until I tell Uncle. You'll be begging for scraps from the street urchins by tomorrow!" She bolted out of the brush towards their stage, scrambled in, and slammed the door.

"Home!" she ordered the driver. "My servant prefers to walk."

Red as a beet, James hollered after her. "At least I won't have to listen to you!"

As he watched the stage disappear down the path, a heavy raindrop hit the middle of his forehead. Two, three, then more dropped until miniature rivers flowed down his face and back. James turned and ran through the pelting rain until he reached the ferry where he bought a ride with some of the change left over from the entrance fee. Once on the Canadian side, he rushed towards the buildings near Table Rock. A bright light and sudden thunderclap split the darkened sky, but in the flash he finally saw it—in a corner of one building and sheltered from the rain— the Signature Album. James scanned the last few pages, waiting for the lightning to illuminate the familiar letters. Nothing. Nothing to do with Tom.

He sighed and stared out into the pouring rain. With his last few coins, he could take the ferry again and return to the Inn, soaked but safe, to resume his servant life. Or he could wander the nearby woods forever and live off grass, insects, and the charity of strangers. Perhaps he could go somewhere else.

TEN

LEGEND OF NIAGARA

THE RAIN HAD STOPPED, BUT THUNDER rumbled in the distance. James leaned against the wooden step under the blanket door, waving away the swarm of tiny insects that nipped at his arms and legs. Kit brought out three dry logs and some kindling. Positioning himself in the middle of the sandy ground he quickly started a warm fire. "This will help keep them away."

"I'm not going back there," said James. "I hate it."

Kit nodded. "I understand but . . ."

"Let me work for you, at least until I save enough to go back to Ireland and find my brother. I'm alone in this country and . . ." His voice trailed off until only the cascade could be heard.

"You can earn the money more quickly at Mr. Green's inn," said Kit. "I cannot pay as much as he."

"I don't care," James declared. "I'll rustle up more visitors than you can count."

Kit smiled. "We can talk in the morning. Rest now."

In the tiny cabin, Kit lay down on a low wooden-platform bed and motioned for James to settle on the thick bearskin across the room. At first, James reveled in the luxurious dark pile, but soon a chilly breeze blew through the blanket door and he shivered like a lost kitten.

"Kit," he said hoarsely. "I'm cold." There was no answer, only Kit's deep snores and the loud rumble of the Falls.

James ran his hands over each upper arm. The insect bites and goosebumps created a rough terrain. James crept around the small cabin, searching for something more than just his red wool coat to keep him warm. In one corner, he touched a large basket covered by a woven straw lid. Perhaps that was where Kit kept his blankets. Rummaging through, James felt something hairy slip through his fingers. Slowly, he pulled it out, handled it for a moment, then shrieked before instantly dropping the object.

"What happened?" mumbled Kit, woken by the high-pitched sound.

"That thing!" said James. "It's a head! You've scalped people, haven't you?"

"I have never scalped anyone, nor do I want to," said Kit as he lifted the object. "What you thought was a scalp is called a False-Face. It is only to be used by the medicine society of my people, in sacred ceremonies to dispel the evil spirits."

James felt the blood rush to his face in embarrassment.

"I do not usually show this to anyone," said Kit. "Wait here." Kit briefly stepped outside and returned with a cloth-wrapped torch lit from the evening's dying fire. In the soft light, James saw that the object was only a wooden mask of a misshapen, peculiar carved face painted black and decorated with long dark horse hair.

"Besides," continued Kit, "any scalping in the past was because the white man offered *rewards* for scalps—I suppose they saw it as a cheap way to fight Indians. And if you were scalped, consider it an honor."

"An honor?"

"Your scalp bestowed your power on the warrior," said Kit. A loud thunderclap broke through the cabin. "Hinu," muttered Kit. "That is the thunder god who lives in the cave behind the Falls." He handed James the horsehair blanket. "Would you like to hear the story?"

James nodded. Rain began to patter on top of the shack and the fire's embers sizzled, but he was no longer cold or afraid.

"It is the legend of Ongniaraha," said Kit.

"Ong-nee-ah-rah-ha," repeated James.

"Yes," said Kit. "That is my people's word for Thunder of the Waters. What your people call Niagara Falls."

James nodded. "And?"

"And legend tells us there was a maiden who was very sad because the people of her village were sick and dying. She wanted to jump off the Falls and leave this world. The thunder god, Hinu, watched her from his cave behind the Falls and saved her life. He said it was the Great Snake who had brought the pain and death to her village. The maiden knew she had to be brave and strong, so she returned to warn her people. They all moved far away. But the Snake tried to follow them. Hinu saw this and fought the Snake. He finally killed it and dashed it against the Falls. The rocks broke off and tumbled to the river below, and that is why there is a great horseshoe shape in the Falls."

"Brave and strong," repeated James glumly. "Those were about the last two words my brother said to me."

Kit lay back down on his wooden bed and stretched. "I suppose I could use a courageous orphan at the tour. Do you still want the job?"

"I sure do," said James without hesitation.

Kit chuckled. "Then you, Master Doyle of the Falls, have a deal."

James's first day of work was busy. He stood near Table Rock, waved a certificate, and called out for tourists to join the tour. His efforts worked. Visitors flocked to the tour like hungry gulls to a fishing boat. James collected their money and took care of the oilcloths. By late afternoon the crowds had begun to thin. As he folded the oilcloths outside, James turned to Kit with a question. "If I am going to work here, shouldn't I actually go on the tour?"

"I wondered when you would ask," replied Kit. He led James down the rickety stairs to the bottom where the plummeting cascade seemed a thousand times more forceful. The once blue-green waters now splashed up wildly into a thick white foam, but it was the ice-cold pelting spray that caught James's breath.

To James's surprise, Kit let him pass. "You can go first," he shouted as they stepped along the wet rocky path.

Halfway through, James halted. Without warning, his foot slipped on a fragment of rock. Luckily, Kit had decided to follow James. He instantly grabbed James's drenched shirt. "Are you all right?"

James managed a nod and steadied his foot on the next flat rock. He became keenly aware of the intense pounding in his chest. A powerful wind gust, silent in the Fall's deafening roar, tore through his clothes. James steadfastly kept his eyes open and did not flinch. If only Tom could see him now.

After several careful steps they reached a jagged ledge that protruded from one side. Straight ahead, the path ended in a sudden descent.

"Termination Rock," shouted James. He stretched out his hand and touched the slimy, wet wall.

He kept his hand there a good long time. A surge of pride welled up inside. *I've done it*, he thought, *I'm brave and strong, like the legend of Kit's people.*

As the summer heat faded, the visitors did as well. So too did James's hope that he would ever save enough money to buy a ticket to Ireland. He checked the Signature Album daily, but never saw Tom's name. Even strangers whom he met, many quite sympathetic to his plight, warned him not to expect any reunion. Back in Ireland, famine had claimed countless lives. If

Tom had never left the country, he might well be among the dead. If he had left, there was a good chance he perished on the voyage over. Many in the overcrowded vessels died. "Coffin ships," they were called, full of the hideous ship fever.

James sat cross-legged on Table Rock, the nubby red wool coat from Mr. Green bundled around him. The sleeves were now too short and the middle tight, but it was still a warm shield against the spray-cooled air near the Falls. A brilliant flurry of red and gold leaves danced off nearby trees, but James remained motionless, resisting any desire to catch one. He gazed over the frothy basin and caught a glimpse near the tour where Kit stood speaking with a young man. Intrigued, James made his way down. He couldn't see the visitor's face but heard his words.

"Are you Kit, the guide?"

James stopped in his tracks. He knew that voice. "Peter!" he cried. "What on earth are you doing here?"

ELEVEN

A DECISION

JAMES WAS SURPRISED TO LEARN THAT Peter now worked as the stable boy at the Niagara Inn—his old job!

"I heard of a contest for boys in Niagara so I came here," explained Peter. "The prize was five dollars and all I had to do was fly a kite across the Gorge."

James snickered. "Let me guess—you didn't win."

"Right," said Peter. "So I decided to head down Ferry Road and that's where I saw Mr. Green and said hello. It took him a moment, but then he recognized me from the orphanage. He said his former stable boy left and offered me a job." Peter tousled James's hair. "So I'm here to find out if the tour has ended for the season." He pulled on imaginary lapels in an impersonation of Mr. Green. "We have guests who wish to experience Termination Rock."

Kit and James laughed. "Bring them along," said Kit as he ushered the boys along the path to his cabin. "Paying customers are always welcome."

James instantly cast about for an excuse not to work that day and avoid coming face to face with Mr.

Green. None came to mind. When they reached Kit's cabin, James finally declared, "I can't believe you work there, Peter. And that Penelope! She parades around like a queen. Expects to be served like one too."

Kit laughed and ducked behind the cabin's blanket door. Peter nodded. "I don't let her get to me. I consider myself a mere *temporary* servant. I'll earn as much money as I can, then I'll leave. How about you? How much do you make at this tour?"

James opened his satchel to reveal the coins he had collected. "My earnings depend on the number of visitors. But I've made quite a lot."

Peter peered at the coins, thought for a moment, then said, "I believe you'll have saved enough to travel back to Ireland in, say, five years."

"Five years?" James frowned. "I'll be old— almost twenty!"

"If you made more like me," added Peter, "it would take less time."

"It's so unfair," said James as he threw a pebble into the brush. "How long until my luck changes?"

Kit emerged from the cabin with a clay pipe. He noticed James's tense expression but didn't say a word. Instead, Kit paused, stared thoughtfully at a hawk gliding overhead, and began to tell a story.

"I remember an old man I once guided on the tour," he said. "At first I refused because he was almost a hundred years old! But the old man insisted. When he came out, there were tears in his eyes. We sat by the fire and talked. I gave him a basket of peaches. He gave me this clay pipe. 'I cannot believe there have been wars near such a beautiful place,' he told me. He said that if *everyone* took the tour, they'd be too happy to think of fighting anymore. That is the power of Ongniaraha."

James immediately cut in. "Ha! Everyone except Penelope."

"She's not that bad," said Peter. "I know Mr. Green will miss her when she returns to Kingston next week."

James looked quizzically at his friend. "You're soft on her, aren't you?"

"No," Peter shot back. "But I've heard her say that she wonders what happened to *you*."

An awkward silence fell over the two boys. James scratched his head, understanding full well what it was like when someone you knew disappeared. He was surprised to learn that Penelope actually thought of him at all.

James threw another pebble up in the air and caught it with one hand. "I suppose anything is possible," he conceded. "If we can one day walk across an ice bridge then maybe Penelope's heart can thaw a little."

"Ice bridge?" asked Peter.

"Sometimes, in a very cold winter," said Kit, "great ice rocks hurtle over the Falls. They form a beautiful frozen bridge that joins these two countries."

James sighed. "Winter also means the ships from Ireland will stop coming over."

"And no visitors at the tour," added Kit. "The

weather grows too dangerous. I spend the winter with my people at the longhouse. You can come with me, or you can stay here and perhaps work for Mr. Green again."

"I don't know," James admitted. He rolled the smooth pebble through his fingers. The thought of working as a servant again made him shudder, but he would need to earn more money soon.

Peter took a quick look at the violet sunset and jumped to his feet. "Mr. Green expects me back at the Inn. I had better return."

James grabbed his satchel. He had made a decision "I'll come with you. Is that okay?"

Peter's face lit up. "Sleep over in the loft. You can leave before dawn."

"I'll stay the night," said James. "But in the morning I plan to speak with Mr. Green."

Peter snored like an iron horse.

James tossed on the sweetly-scented straw and breathed deeply. The stable was warm and familiar, but he couldn't sleep. Even clutching the little sheepskin goat didn't help. He scratched a bug bite and mulled over his decision. In a few hours, he would ask Mr. Green for temporary employment. Steady work throughout the winter, a couple of months at the tour, and then he would buy a ticket back to Ireland. *Mr. Green is compassionate*, thought James. *And he knows what Penelope was like. A rare Englishman, surely he would understand how things got out of hand that day at the caravan.*

James sat up. Sleep would assuredly not be his companion tonight. He was too alert, too awake.

A horse whinnied into the still night air while pigs snorted loudly. James listened to their sounds. *Do the animals have trouble sleeping tonight, too?* The last time he had heard such complaining was back in Ireland. Moments before the torches had ignited his family's home, the animals knew. It was as if they sensed what was about to happen.

James bit his lip and decided to copy Tom's name again. He didn't need to; he knew each letter by heart. But he had to do something, anything to stop those frightful memories. He pulled up his satchel, took out the journal, and reached for an oil lamp. The slight sway extinguished the tiny flame; the lamp was now out of oil. James rubbed and scratched his legs until the swollen red bumps started to ooze blood. He was miserable.

He tapped Peter on the shoulder. "I need oil," he whispered. "There should be a jarful on the shelves just inside the servants' quarters. Can you fetch me some?"

Peter groaned. James nudged him harder.

"You get it," mumbled Peter as he pulled the blanket up to his chin and rolled over.

"But I don't want anyone to see me yet," whispered James. Peter did not reply.

James shook his head. *I'll have to do it myself.* He climbed down the loft and headed towards the servants' quarters for the oil. At the entrance, James stopped suddenly. A distinct odor wafted through the air. The pungent smell of smoke.

James dashed back to the stable and scampered up to the loft. "Peter!" he said, shaking his friend. "You've got to come with me. I think there's a fire!"

"Fire?" Peter repeated as he rubbed his eyes. "Where?"

James shimmied down the ladder. "At the Inn. Come on!"

The boys raced towards the main house. The fiery smell grew stronger in the night air.

"Where is it coming from?" asked Peter.

"I don't know," said James. "You take the main entrance. I'll check below stairs."

Peter scurried around the corner. James headed to the servants' quarters, opened the kitchen door, and stepped into a thick haze. "Wake up!" he shouted through the kitchen. "Fire!"

He dashed through the rest of the quarters and bolted up the stairs. Flames darted out from the study where James glimpsed a pile of newspapers ablaze.

"Fire!" he screamed at the top of his lungs.

A thick black cloud circled above him and his throat instantly tightened. Knowing the air near the floor was cooler, James crept towards the door. He was about to push it open when he jerked back his hand. It was like touching red-hot coals; the fire was behind the door. He would have to go the other way.

By now, footsteps and shouts echoed through the courtyard. Above them he heard Mr. Green shout, "My pipe! Oh heavens! Fire! Fire in the study!"

"Water!" ordered Cook. "Buckets of water! Quick!"

James followed the voices and crawled blindly through the heavy blanket of smoke. He stopped abruptly. Something prickly had stepped on his hand; something wet nuzzled his cheek.

"Fritz!" he yelled between coughs. The poodle whimpered as James snatched him up. He tucked the dog under one arm and continued until a wave of cool air filled his aching lungs. Two people rushed ahead to the open door, jostling James along until he too was finally outside, sprawled on the courtyard stone, coughing violently. In an instant, the dog leaped out of his grasp.

Mr. Green caught the frightened animal. "What the devil . . . James?" he said helping the boy up. "I'm shocked to see you here!"

James took a deep breath and scanned the scene. It was a strange sight. Wealthy guests in dressing gowns stood stunned beside frazzled servants. After a few seconds of bewildered silence, every available hand—not just those of servants—passed sloshing buckets of water to douse the flames.

"Where's Peter?" asked James.

"I saw him assisting Mr. Hodge," replied Mr. Green "Here he comes now."

Mr. Hodge rushed towards his employer and panted, "All accounted for, sir."

"But where is Penelope?" pleaded Mr. Green, his eyes darting left and right. "I shall never forgive myself for leaving that lit pipe in the study if . . ."

"Fritz!" cried a voice behind the crowds. It was

Penelope, pushing her way through and running towards them. "Uncle, you found him!" She grabbed her poodle and hugged him tightly.

Cook emerged from the bucket line, wiping her sweaty brow. "The fire's tamed," she told Mr. Green. "Thanks to James's warnings. No telling what might have happened without him, sir."

Mr. Green turned to his niece. "It was James who found your precious pet, not I. He saved the Inn."

Penelope slowly lowered her eyes. Her eyelashes batted like black butterfly wings. "Thank you so much, Master Doyle," she whispered, eyes still downcast.

TWELVE

BROTHERS

EVEN THOUGH A FULL WEEK HAD PASSED since the fire, a smoky odor still lingered in the parlor. From his seat on the rich brocade furniture, James stared across at the window's heavy drapes that were the color of stewed prunes. Why had Mr. Green asked him here? And why was he permitted to wait on the chesterfield? Servants never sat in the parlor room.

Nonetheless, James knew much had changed. Penelope's overt politeness remained almost unbelievable. He was equally pleased and surprised by Mr. Green's boundless generosity. Not only did Mr. Green hire him back, he agreed to provide leave during the summer so James could assist Kit at the tour. Who would have thought an Englishman could be so kind? *I know I can make enough money to find Tom now*, thought James.

Just then, a soft whistle distracted him.

"Psst . . . you won't believe this."

James spun his head around and saw Peter at the doorway, a broad smile across his face and a crumpled newspaper in one hand.

"It's *The New York Herald*," whispered Peter. "You're famous."

He skulked into the parlor and crouched behind the chesterfield. In a low voice, he read a short paragraph on the first page:

Stable boy alerts guests in Niagara Inn fire.

Young James Doyle, an orphaned Irish immigrant, saved the lives of numerous guests of the Niagara Inn—owned by the well-known Mr. Green. Plucky Master Doyle smelled smoke and discovered the study on fire. His quick and brave actions awoke the sleeping guests, permitting them to escape the fiery blaze. With the help of the other servants and the Inn's guests, the fire was quickly doused. Mr. Green would like to add that damage to the Inn was slight.

"Cook has prepared a great big meal in celebration," added Peter. "All the servants are ready to thank you—the Inn's hero."

James chuckled. So that was why Mr. Green had asked him to wait in the parlor—he wanted to announce the surprise below stairs.

James was about to open his mouth when Peter hushed him up and tiptoed away. Someone was coming.

Mr. Green entered the parlor with Penelope on one arm. James stood. "My dear niece," Mr. Green said. "Please fetch our guest."

James was confused. "Sir?"

Mr. Green brought his fingers to his lips and

smiled mysteriously. Penelope skipped off only to return a moment later. "Here he is," she grinned and stepped aside, revealing the guest.

"Tom!"

Half laughing, half crying, James leaped into his brother's open arms. He tried to hold back the tears, but they raced down his face as surely as water fell over the Falls. "I was going back," sobbed James. "Back to Ireland to find you."

Tom's voice cracked with emotion. "We are together again," he whispered. After a long embrace, Tom placed his large hands on James's shoulders and said, "Let me look at you, you've grown."

"I'm almost as tall as you," chortled James. He wiped the tears from his cheeks.

Tom smiled, then nodded towards Mr. Green. "And you'll keep growing, right alongside me. Your generous employer has already spoken with me. He has offered us work here for the winter. In the summer, Peter will join us and we can help Kit at the tour. We will be together, brothers of the Falls."

James squeezed Tom's hand. "Kit agrees?"

"Ask him yourself. He's downstairs."

A tingling sensation shot through James. He blinked repeatedly, ready to awaken from his pleasant dream. But this was not an illusion. Tom, his skin tanned a deep bronze and his face framed by dark brown waves and a matching beard that made him look like their father, was big as life. They were finally together again.

Mr. Green cleared his throat. "I don't wish to

interrupt this happy reunion, but we should proceed now. I do believe a sumptuous meal awaits the guests of honor."

Below stairs, a tremendous cheer greeted the brothers.

"A toast to our James!" hollered Peter. "If it weren't for his brave actions, his name would not have been in the newspaper and his brother might have never known he was here!"

"That," replied James, "we call the luck of the Irish!" The room erupted in laughter. James raised his glass. "And praise for Peter," he said, gesturing towards his friend. "Consider yourself 'Peter Doyle' for as long as you wish. You have been like a brother to me and I will always be grateful."

Peter looked stunned. "Me? A Doyle?"

"You have my oath of loyalty," James assured him.

"Here, here!" cheered Tom, and everyone clapped. Cook placed the roast duck on the table. As they ate, Tom recounted his own incredible story. The guests soaked up every word, every detail of how he had remained in Liverpool after their separation, how he worked his fingers to the bone, finally saving enough money for a new ticket to America to find his little brother. Touched, Cook hugged James and Tom, the servants dabbed at their watery eyes, and even Mr. Hodge managed a small crooked smile.

After the meal, they headed outside and gathered around a fire where Kit heated corn kernels until they popped into fluffy, bite-sized treats. Everyone ate, talked, and sang into the night. Hours later, only the three brothers remained beside the smoldering fire.

Tom stood up and stretched. "Time for shut-eye. There is much to be done tomorrow."

"Such as our writing lessons?" asked James.

"Yes, most definitely add those," interrupted Peter.

Tom laughed and winked in agreement. He turned towards James. "This will be my first good night's sleep. I could have used your little sheepskin goat for these past seven months," he joked.

James picked up the nearby rain bucket and threw what remained inside on the fire. The burning embers snapped and hissed briefly before their orange-red glow disappeared into the dark. James put down the bucket and grinned. "The goat?" he said as he walked with Tom towards the stable loft. "You can have it. I haven't needed it for ages."

Historical Postscript

The trickle of immigrants into America during the early 1800s became a flood by mid-century. Most departed from ports such as Liverpool, England, hoping to escape poverty. Many were Irish immigrants who grew grains for absentee landlords but subsisted on their own small potato crops. In 1845, a change in the weather introduced a devastating new disease to Ireland's potato crop. Without potatoes, the principal food source for the majority of Ireland's inhabitants, the population was devastated by famine for the next six years. The poor had little choice: leave or starve.

It was a difficult journey for all. Historical records show that some families were accidentally separated, much like Thomas and James. Others perished on overcrowded ships during the often long and dangerous voyage. The immigrants had to be strong to survive.

Imagine their thoughts when they stepped foot on American soil. Here was a vast country of trees, land, and flourishing new towns. For those whose journey brought them to Niagara Falls, the sight and sound must have made an incredible impression.

For centuries the First Peoples—the Native Indians—had been the only humans to set eyes on the "thundering waters." It wasn't until 1697 that a European, a missionary priest named Father Louis Hennepin, first wrote about an "incredible waterfall, which has no equal."

The characters in this book are fictional but their stories are based in actual history. Visitors did engrave dates into trees beside the Falls and sign their names in a "signature album." They hired guides and paid for a "Journey Behind the Great Falling Sheet of Water to Termination Rock" tour and certificate. The "Niagara Inn" of this story is modeled after Cataract House (later the Eagle Tavern), built in 1815 on the American side of the Falls by General Parkhurst Whitney. Several years later, Canadian William Forsyth erected his "Pavilion" and offered trips down to a cavern behind the Falls. In 1827, the two entrepreneurs even organized a strange (and cruel) stunt. An old schooner, the *Michigan*, was filled with various animals and sent over the Falls. One bear managed to escape at the river, but only a goose survived the actual plunge.

Two years later, a forty-foot tall stone observation tower was built at Terrapin Point on Goat Island. Until its demolition in 1873, Terrapin Tower offered tourists a thrilling view of the Horseshoe Falls. It can still be seen in famous paintings such as the seven-foot-tall masterpiece by Frederick Edwin Church, first exhibited in New York City in 1847.

The Erie Canal opened on October 26, 1825. At

363 miles long, 40 feet wide, and 4 feet deep, it cut travel time from the East Coast (Hudson River) to the Great Lakes in half. Tourism to the Falls increased, and many people, including the famous writer Nathaniel Hawthorne, flocked to this magnificent place. With the advent of steamships and railways, it became fashionable to see the Falls first-hand—and even spend honeymoons there!

A kite-flying contest really was held in 1847 near the Whirlpool Rapids. The winner was a boy named Homan Walsh who managed to fly his kite, which carried a light rope, across the Niagara Gorge onto the American side. This rope was used to haul heavier ropes and eventually steel cables across the river to commence construction of a suspension bridge. Sam Patch did perform one of the earliest death-defying stunts at Niagara by diving into the turbulent Niagara River. The first person to survive a trip over the Falls in a wooden barrel was Annie Taylor in 1901. Numerous stunts, both successful and unsuccessful, have been performed since. Perhaps the most miraculous case was that of seven-year-old Roger Woodward. On July 9, 1960, the boat he was in capsized and Roger accidentally plunged over the Falls. The only protection he wore was a life jacket. Somehow, he survived, suffering only a mild, temporary concussion. Forty-three years later, a Michigan man named Kirk Jones became the only person to survive a plunge over Niagara Falls without a safety device. Jones said he jumped into the Horseshoe Falls because he was depressed after losing his job.

HISTORICAL POSTSCRIPT

When he emerged unhurt, he said he realized he had made a terrible mistake and was lucky to be alive.

Today, some 12 million visitors from all over the world come to Niagara each year. While some of the scenery has changed and the force of the waterfall has been diminished by half for electrical power, Niagara Falls nonetheless remains an impressive experience. Along with the first Natives, explorers, or even immigrant orphans such as James, those who visit the Falls leave with feelings of awesome wonder and reverence for nature. As a plaque mounted nearby indicates, it is hoped that peoples of all nations will take with them this new understanding, ultimately bringing peace throughout the world.

HISTORICAL POSTSCRIPT

NIAGARA FACTS

- The Falls, Niagara River, and Gorge were formed after the last ice age, about 12,000 years ago.
- Niagara Falls consists of the American Falls, the Horseshoe Falls, and a smaller Bridal Veil Falls (separated from the American Falls by Luna Island).
- American Falls is about 184 feet high and 900 feet (three football fields) wide. As the name suggests, American Falls is American waters.
- Bridal Veil Falls is about 181 feet high and 56 feet wide. Located between Luna Island and Goat Island, this is also American waters.
- Horseshoe Falls, about 176 feet high and approximately 2,200 feet (seven football fields) wide, is 99 percent Canadian waters.

GLOSSARY

berth – a built-in bed or bunk on a ship or train
Black fever – a disease known today as typhus
cataract – a large waterfall
packet – a boat that travels on a regular route
precipice – a rock face that is straight up or overhangs
privy – a water closet; toilet
rosary – a series of prayers
satchel – a small carrying bag, usually with a shoulder strap
snuff – powdered tobacco sniffed through the nose
stage or *wagon* – a horse-drawn coach
trundle bed – a small, pull-out bed stored underneath a larger bed

OTHER BOOKS OF INTEREST

- Denenberg, Barry. *The Diary of Mary Driscoll, an Irish Mill Girl, Lowell, Massachusetts, 1847*. New York: Scholastic, 1997.
- Friedman, Russell. *Immigrant Kids*. Illinois: Scott Foresman, 1995.
- Harness, Cheryl. *The Amazing, Impossible Erie Canal*. New York: Aladdin Paperbacks, 2001.
- Whitcraft, Melissa. *The Niagara River*. London: Franklin Watts, Inc., 2001.